BILLY BLUE GOAT'S RANCH STORIES FOR KIDS

No Ifs, Ands, or 'Butts' About It

By Elissa Mae Phillips

ISBN-13: 978-1725936874

DEDICATION

I dedicate this illustrated book of children's stories of ranch life
to my children, grandchildren, and future generations.

Elissa Mae Phillips

Table of Contents

A Dangerous Ride

My name is Billy Blue Goat and I like to take care of cows, horses and other ranch animals. Ranch life is a great life for 'kids' of all kinds, but when I was a very young goat, I found out how hazardous ranch life can be. Goats like to jump and climb on anything and everything. That is just our nature. This habit almost finished me off at a very young age.

I had been purchased and given to a little girl named Sarah. She lives on a ranch near Ancho, New Mexico with her parents, Becca and Matt, and her big brother Joel. Sarah and Joel were their dad's very able cowhands.

Joel was school age and Sarah was not. One fine day, Joel caught the school bus and left little Sarah to go with her dad to check on the cattle's watering tanks. Most ranches now have electric water pumps, but windmills still play a big part in pumping tank water. You would not have the deer and the antelope 'roaming' without ranchers taking care of their pastures, fixing water tanks, and controlling predators.

A pipeline runs from a big storage tank that is filled from one deep well. Then it goes to all nine watering tanks on the ranch. These are scattered over seventeen sections of land. For those who don't know, a section of land is 640 acres, or one square mile. Because New Mexico is so dry and doesn't grow a lot of grass, it takes about fifty acres of land to feed one cow for a year. Water is of major importance since each cow or horse drinks between ten and thirty gallons of water each day, depending on the temperature.

That morning, Matt was pulling a trailer behind his pickup truck and that looked like a fun ride to me. I jumped into the trailer to take a ride, but Matt happened to see me, and he put me back out. Then he and little Sarah started off again. I must tell you that goats are very hard headed (just like some people I know). So, just as they pulled away, I hopped back into the trailer and was bouncing along just fine until Matt hit a big bump and I flew out of that trailer like a bird!

I hit the ground very hard just as little Sarah happened to look out the back window of the pickup.

She cried out, and her dad stopped and rescued me. At first, they thought I had broken a leg, but it was just badly sprained and was very sore for a while.

This experience taught me that ranch life can be a real challenge. And there are no ifs, ands, or 'butts' about it!

Elissa Phillips

A New Home

This is Billy Blue Goat to tell you that after my trailer experience, my owner, little Sarah, was very concerned for my safety. She told her dad that she wanted to take me to her grandparent's place where I could be safe.

Her grandparents had a fifty-acre place with good water and a permanent pasture that fed about a dozen cows and two horses. They were willing to take me, so Matt and Sarah hauled me sixty miles to the new place, which I soon learned was called Walnut Grove. I also learned to call Sarah's grandparents Mama Lisa and Big Daddy.

There was one problem. Big Daddy had a very big, harlequin Great Dane named Zorro. This Dane did not think a goat was a good addition to his big, fenced in yard! When Matt and Sarah put me in the yard, the rodeo began! I took one look at Zorro and ran for my life! Zorro took one look at me and the chase was on! Matt, Sarah and Big Daddy were all yelling at Zorro to stop, but I wasn't counting on that!

Goats are very sure-footed, and I spotted two big propane tanks placed side by side. These tanks supplied gas for the kitchen and other stoves. I was going very fast when I leaped on top of the first tank. My hooves slid across and I ended up stuck between the two tanks. What a commotion that caused! Zorro was running after me and barking. Matt, Sarah, and Big Daddy were yelling and running after both of us.

Matt is a big man. He lifted me out from between the tanks and held Zorro away from me. Big Daddy then held onto Zorro, while Matt set me down and tried to introduce us properly. That did not go over very well, since I decided to butt Zorro head on! That took him by surprise and I had him bluffed for a short while. We finally formed and uneasy truce.

In the yard there were two very big rocks shaped like tables, and these became my place of refuge. When Zorro would start playing too rough with me, I could climb on top of the rocks and butt him from that perch to ward him off.

For me, life at Walnut Grove would be a big adventure, and little Sarah was happy to know I was safe. And there are no ifs, ands, or 'butts' about it!

Elissa Phillips

Coyotes in the Pasture

I was soon given the run of the permanent pasture at Walnut Grove instead of the yard. And I became friends with two very big animals. My two very important pals were a huge, red bull named Tuffy and an equally large, longhorn steer named Tex New Mex.

This all came about because one night I chose to sleep in the pasture instead of the yard. I was enjoying the cool air when I was awakened by the howling of a pack of coyotes. They were hungry and hunting game for dinner. Zorro, the great Dane, could hear them too and began howling from the yard. However, he was fenced in and could not keep me safe.

The coyotes were coming into the pasture and I was very afraid. I could see Tuffy and Tex New Mex standing not too far from where I was, so I ran to get between them just as the coyote pack spotted me and headed my way. I was really scared now, and I wouldn't be surprised if my long, stiff hair wasn't standing straight up on my back. To my great relief, Tex New Mex put his big long horns down and swung them back and forth. Then big Tuffy put his huge head down and dared the coyotes to come any closer. The coyotes decided to hunt for easier game and they left our pasture in a hurry.

I learned I could not have any better friends than my two protectors. Now every night I sleep where they are close by. And there are no ifs, ands or 'butts' about it!

Elissa Phillips

New Calves

This is Billy Blue Goat to tell you what I know about life on a ranch.

Every year from May until October, ranch bulls are turned out of their pastures and get to share the pastures with the cows. Once October arrives, the bulls are moved back into their own pastures. Everyone is waiting for the year's new calf crop which usually arrives in late February and March of the following year.

The mama cows always seem to have their new calves when stormy weather brings in cold rain or snow. The new calves meet the world wet and cold, but the mama cows lick them clean and get them to drinking warm milk right away.

Human babies are totally helpless at birth, but baby calves can get right up on their wobbly legs and seem to know where their dinner is waiting for them. Mama cows are very protective of their calves, and I learned to keep my distance till we could all get acquainted.

All new calves are cute and frisky, but I really like the Herefords best with their little white faces and red shiny bodies. Calves like to stick together, and they will run and play and kick up their heels. They are really fun to watch.

You will see one mama cow being their baby sitter while the other mama cows graze or go to drink water, but they don't leave their calves for long. When a mama moos, each calf knows which 'moo' is calling them.

A ranch cannot survive without a new calf crop each year, so it is the big event of the year. And there are no ifs, ands, or 'butts' about it!

The Roundup

This is Billy Blue Goat to tell you the new calves, along with all the cows are rounded up so the calves can be ear marked, branded, and vaccinated. This is done for their health and protection, and to help keep them from being stolen from their mamas. The branding does not hurt them for long because their mamas quickly lick the new brands and get the calves settled down. Then they are all turned back out to the pastures until time for the fall roundup.

A few calves, that might be born later, will be branded by Matt as he makes his regular rides over the ranch checking on all the cows.

I know Sarah and her big brother Joel always look forward to the fall round-up because their cousins, aunts, uncles, and some neighbors from other ranches all come to help. Everyone pitches in by gathering and separating the herd. Some of the cows and calves will stay on the ranch, while others will be shipped to their new owner.

The ranch ladies always set up Dutch ovens so that lunch will be served. These are heavy, lidded, iron pots that they fill with biscuits, beef, and beans and place on hot coals to cook for all the hungry cowboys and cowgirls. Sarah always saves me a couple of biscuits, which she knows I love. There is a lot of laughter and everyone enjoys the event even though it is a lot of hard and dusty work.

This is the time of year that the ranch makes its money to operate the for the year ahead. Big trucks arrive and lots of cattle are loaded onto them. They will go live with the people who have purchased them from the ranch. Though it is sad to see them go, the ranch could not survive without selling their yearly crop of cows. The rest of the cows are turned back to pasture for the winter and the ranch cycle starts all over again. And there are no ifs, ands or 'butts' about it!

Winter on the Ranch

This is Billy Blue Goat to tell you about winter on the ranch. You would think it would be a time to just sit by the fire and eat popcorn and drink hot chocolate, but that doesn't happen very often.

Joel and Sarah are old enough and are up very early doing their chores. First, they feed some sheep at the barn, then go to the chicken coup and feed the chickens, and then they feed the dogie calves, if there are any.

In case you don't know what a dogie calf is, it is a calf that has lost its' mother for some reason and has to be fed by hand. This requires mixing up a powdered milk formula and putting it in a big bottle with a big, rubber nipple attached. The calf quickly learns to drink from it, and Sarah or Joel must do this at least twice a day until it can be weaned. Just like a human baby, it takes about four to six months until a calf no longer requires milk. Then it can eat grass. You can see, feeding a dogie can become a real job.

After chores, Joel and Sarah hurry back to eat breakfast and get ready to go with their mom, Becca, to school. Becca teaches at their school and they must drive four miles from their house, on a dirt road, just to get to the paved road. Then they continue for another sixteen more miles to school. They are always glad if the dirt road is not boggy so they don't have to ride in a four wheel drive vehicle.

Their dad, Matt, also went out early to make the rounds to the ranch water tanks. These must be checked daily to break any ice that may have formed in the night so that the cows will have water to drink. If it is really cold, he may have to go out again before dark and break the ice again. If there is snow on the ground, he will throw out hay or cubes from the back of the pickup for the cows and horses to eat. The cows and horses learn quickly there might be eats in that truck, and they all run to meet him when they hear it coming. This makes it a lot easier to get them all fed.

Each day is a long day for Joel and Sarah. Often, they have ball practice or a ball game to play after school. This means it is after dark by the time they get back home and chores still need to be done in the cold with lanterns or flashlights. Their family then gathers for supper followed by any homework that must be done.

You can see that ranch life creates a full-time job for the whole family. And there are no ifs, ands, or 'butts' about it!

13

Ducklings in the Pond

This is Billy Blue Goat to tell you that my first owner had to do a certain procedure to keep me from growing horns before she could sell me to Sarah's dad.

My procedure did not quite do the job it was supposed to do, and as I grew, the two horns also grew. They just did not grow in the normal way! One horn was hollow and finally broke off when I butted things. The other grew in a peculiar turn and made me look quite comical as you can tell by my pictures.

After I came to live at Big Daddy's place, I learned if I would 'butt' the front gate of the yard, it would make a big racket and Mama Lisa would bring me out a small bowl of animal cookies, which I dearly love. I would quickly nibble them all up, and then I had to hurry back to the pasture to look after my cows.

One particular morning, before I could finish my cookies, I saw Mr. Matt drive up in his pickup with Joel and Sarah. They all got out and proceeded to take a big cage out of the pickup bed. In it were eleven very cute ducklings.

Since I am naturally curious, I had to see what this was all about. I followed Big Daddy and Mama Lisa to our pond which is near their house. On the pond lived a beautiful big drake that had recently lost his two other ducks to predators. Mama Lisa had asked Mr. Matt to try to bring some new ducklings for the pond so the drake would not be so lonely.

When they got the cage to the edge of the pond, Joel and Sarah opened the cage door and pushed the ducklings out into the water. They were beautiful to see and we all watched as the big drake spotted them and began to swim swiftly toward them. We all thought he would be delighted, but his reaction came as a big shock!

He immediately attacked the first ducking he came to and proceeded to push the duckling's head under water with his big beak, clearly intending to drown it! Everyone began to yell and throw sticks at the drake. One stick found the mark and drove the drake away before he could kill the little duckling. Immediately he circled and began to attack another one, and everyone had to drive him away again.

It took some doing with everyone getting good and wet, but finally Mr. Matt captured him and placed him in the ducklings' cage. He would have to be transferred to a different pond back at Matt's ranch!

All the new ducklings got over their fright and happily accepted Mama Lisa's pond as their new home.

We were all sorry the drake had to be taken away, but animals' reactions can be a big surprise. They are sometimes hard to understand, but I am sure it makes perfect sense to them. And there are no ifs, ands, or 'butts' about it!

15

Taking Care of the Animals

This is Billy Blue Goat to tell you that ranch 'kids' learn to take care of animals at an early age.

The schools in our area have programs to teach 'kids' how to do that in the very best ways. There is FFA, which stands for 'Future Farmers of America', as well as FHA, which stands for 'Future Homemakers of America'.

The 'kids' can choose to learn to raise different farm or ranch animals for their projects, or they might choose to learn home skills such as sewing, baking, crafts or gardening. They can learn to judge animals, or how to identify and process meats.

There are also classes available to teach them how to repair equipment and weld, which can really come in handy for either a farm or a ranch. Those skills really help hold down the cost and keep everything working.

Each year, counties and states have their fairs where all the products of the 'kids' hard work are displayed. There are judging events that give ribbons and prize money to the different participants. I love to go in the animal barns to see all the small pens of lambs, goats, cows, chickens, different birds and other farm animals.

The 'kids', who show their animals, must wash and trim them. They also must keep their pens clean with plenty of food and water. When each one's turn comes to show their animal, it becomes apparent if they have trained their animal to lead and stand still for the judges. That is important to show that they have spent the needed time working with their animals. Showmanship is one of the categories they are judged on, and there is a special ribbon given for that.

The last day brings the big event. It is an auction where the winning animals are sold to the highest bidders. That is a bitter-sweet moment, because the 'kids' have become very attached to their animals. All participants knew this would happen and had accepted that part of their project before they ever started.

Many local businesses bid to increase the amount of the purchase price so the 'kids' are well rewarded for their year of hard work. The money they earn is often reinvested in another animal to raise, or saved to help pay for college.

Once the fair is over, everyone pitches in to clean the fair barns and leave them as clean as they found them. All the families return to their farms and ranches to begin a new year of raising animals and food products that our nation depends upon. It requires a lot of hard work, but I think it is a rewarding and wonderful family life for all those who choose to be our ranchers and farmers. And there are no ifs, ands, or 'butts' about it.

Ranchers Are Not Dummies

This is Billy Blue Goat to tell you that ranchers and cowboys are not Dummies!

Some people seem to think so. That means I need to teach people about what knowledge and education our ranchers and cowboys must acquire to run a productive ranch. By being productive, I mean a ranch that can hopefully make them a living, as well as supplying vital goods to our nation.

I have made a list and there are probably subjects I haven't thought of.

* Animal Science. That means knowing the physical make-up of different animals, their different needs and the care required.

* Grain and seed identification. This is important for the feeding requirements of different animals.

* Local plant identification. The ranchers need to know the good plants from the noxious weeds that must be controlled so the animals are not poisoned.

* Soil and water conservation methods. Soil and water make the plants grow and allow the animals to eat and drink.

* How many animals to put on the ranch. That depends on the soil, the types of native grasses, water availability, and climate. Overstocking is bad for the land and the animals. It will make the rancher lose money.

* Accounting, business management, and marketing. Without a good working knowledge of all three areas, the ranchers would soon be out of business.

* Maintenance skills. There are lots of things that can break down and need repair on a ranch or farm. The rancher can't afford to drive many miles and pay lots of money for repairs. He needs basic knowledge in skills like welding, plumbing, electrical repairs, and equipment maintenance.

Many small ranchers do much of their own work, but larger ranches may have a ranch foreman and extra cowboys who will need to be trained. Many ranchers and ranch workers have college educations that cover a variety of needs for successful ranch operations.

If you really want to know what ranching or farming is about, I would suggest you hire on as a ranch hand for at least one summer. This will be a great education in itself!

My ranch stories are to help inform you that there is a lot more to being a rancher or a cowboy than wearing a big hat, cowboy boots, and spurs. And there are no ifs, ands, or 'butts' about it!

How To Train A Cowboy

This is Billy Blue Goat to tell you how to train a Cowboy! This story relates how Great Granddad trained a greenhorn who wanted to be a Cowboy.

I must first tell you a greenhorn is a person who knows nothing about the job at hand! He must be taught all about how to do the job.

This particular young man was an Easterner who had come out West for the adventure, and with a romantic view of what it meant to be a Cowboy!

Great Granddad was the foreman for the very large ranch located in Lincoln County, New Mexico. The ranch was called, Dollar Mark 11 Ranch, and its' brand looked like this: $11. This young greenhorn asked the ranch owner for a job as a cowboy. The owner decided to try him out by sending him to train under Great Granddad.

The next day he presented himself for the job. Great Granddad had him join him in his old, battered jeep along with a tin coffee can, a pick and a shovel. They went on a long, very rough ride up in the hills to an old fence line that obviously needed major repair. Great Granddad had the young man unload the coffee can, pick and shovel and some new cedar posts. He then handed him a pair of gloves. He told him to dig out the old broken posts and replace them with the new ones and he would return and pick him up later in the day.

The young man asked, "What is the coffee can for?" Great Granddad said, "When you start to dig and clean out the postholes for the new posts, there will be so many rocks that you will need the can to get them out."

The romantic picture of becoming a cowboy faded very quickly for the young man, but he did stick it out and got the job done. Eventually, he got to learn to ride and help with the cows. He also found out that there are a lot of hard, dirty jobs that go with the title of 'Cowboy'. We can all learn from these short stories. It may take a lot of hard work using that small coffee can, but work will help us achieve our goals and fulfill our purpose in life. And there are no ifs, ands, or 'butts' about it!

Made in the USA
Columbia, SC
19 September 2018